The Innkeeper's Wife

A TIMELESS NATIVITY STORY BY

SAVANNAH JEZOWSKI

THE INNKEEPER'S WIFE

FOR NICOLE K. AND ANNIE P.

CHAPTER ONE

SNOW DRIFTED FROM the sky, heavy snowflakes that gathered quickly on the frozen ground already sporting the remnants of a previous snowfall. Ginny Latham stood behind the service desk within the safety of Timeless Bed & Breakfast's lobby and squinted into the gathering darkness.

The snow had been getting increasingly worse as the day progressed. They'd already received at least eight or nine inches, and projections indicated the accumulation would continue throughout the night and through Christmas, growing worse before the blizzard broke.

Talk about a White Christmas.

Ginny's mouth turned down into a frown. Of course, it meant more work for her. With all of the guests stranded due to inclement weather, she'd be struggling to entertain them until they could resume their planned holiday activities…and there were a lot of folks to entertain. Because it was Christmas Eve, the B&B was completely booked. Timeless did well throughout the year, but especially well on holidays. City folks seemed to like the secluded setting in the woods surrounding Houghton Lake, Michigan.

Ginny had liked vacationing here too until her husband got the bright idea to go into the hotel business, emptied their investment portfolio, and bought this run-down mansion in the middle of nowhere. Now she labored away so other people could enjoy their vacations.

She slammed her scheduling book closed with an annoyed huff. They hadn't been on a vacation in three years. Not that it mattered. They didn't have any kids to worry about, and she was a big girl and didn't need pampering.

The lie stabbed deep, stirring up that perpetual ache in the pit of her stomach.

Footsteps clomped down the hall from the kitchen before Caleb's dark auburn curls and broad shoulders appeared. He ripped off his gloves and blew on his fingers as he approached the counter. He was pushing six feet and just a little on the plump side, although no one but Ginny had probably noticed his slow weight gain over the past couple of years. She'd even been finding some gray in his dark hair. Middle age was catching up to them.

To the both of them.

Her hand trembled slightly before she pressed her palm flat against the countertop.

Caleb shrugged out of his overcoat and ruffled his curls to dislodge snow all over her hardwood floors. "Brr! It's brutal out there!" he announced, casting her a smile. His cheeks were bright red, breath coming in heavy gasps from his workout. "Guess all the boys and girls are going to get their White Christmas this year."

Ginny's mouth pulled down even farther as he unwittingly mirrored her own thoughts just moments before. She wished he hadn't mentioned all the boys and girls. Didn't he care? Didn't he know what such a comment would do to her? Especially on the holidays?

She turned away before he could see the hurt spreading across her cheeks.

"I shoveled and threw some more salt down, but I doubt anyone will be out there until the storm breaks. They're saying we could get another foot by Tuesday."

Oh joy.

She shoved her register into its place in the crowded filing cabinet. She had no choice but to turn back to face him. Not that it mattered: he leaned one hip against the counter, his attention on the bank of windows and the snow streaking by rather than on her. She took a moment to linger on his face, on the deep-set blue eyes that had first attracted her back when they were in college. His dimples were more pronounced now, thanks to the added pounds over the past fifteen years.

Thirty-five.

Was she really going to be thirty-five in January? Her internal clock ticked away like a time bomb about to explode.

"I'm thinking I need to get a snowblower," Caleb continued, still out of breath. "I know, I know what you're going to say—it's an unnecessary expense that a little elbow grease can take care of for free."

Ginny shot him an annoyed look, mostly because he was right: that was exactly what she would say. He grinned at her, like a child asking for an early Christmas present.

Another pang stabbed her. "You don't need a snowblower," she muttered. "What about my stove? If that thing bites the dust, how am I going to serve breakfast?"

Her husband exhaled in a disappointed huff. "You're right. Of course, you need the stove first. It's just…a snowblower…"

"Is a fancy new toy you don't need."

"Precisely." He beamed at her as if he'd somehow won the discussion.

Avoiding his cheeky grin, she made herself busy straightening things he had knocked askew throughout the day. The stapler had been moved, sticky notes plastered about with reminders and questions for her, pens and highlighters littered across the counter. Candy Cane wrappers. A water ring from his coffee cup. No, three water rings from his first, second, and third cups of coffee.

Frustrated, she shoved things back into place. Then she began to rip the sticky notes off one by one, most of them filled with unnecessary reminders or rambling musings.

Don't forget to thaw the turkey.

Put ice salt on the shopping list.

Turned away three more guests today…maybe we should expand next year.

She snatched up the last sticky note, a neon pink one stuck to the monitor of her computer. Her hand froze, hovering in midair as she read the last note, scrawled in her husband's sloppy cursive.

I love you, Ginny-girl.

She lifted her gaze and found him staring at her, a smile turning his lips that did nothing to conceal the furrow between his eyebrows and the concern in his blue-jean hued eyes. She opened her mouth to tell him she loved him too, but the words stuck in her throat for some reason.

She did love him, loved him so much she ached with feeling, but there were days when she couldn't say it. Admitting she had feelings only made her that much more aware of the pain she kept hidden away where no one could see it.

No one but Caleb, that was. He saw through her as if her carefully established walls were fragile panes of glass. One tap and the whole façade would crash down around her ears.

Which was probably why he tip-toed around with that wrinkle between his eyes ninety-nine percent of the time.

His gaze flicked away suddenly, to the window. Ginny followed the direction of his eyes as headlights bobbed in the darkness.

"Holy smokes, who's out on a night like this?" he exclaimed as he pulled his overcoat off the counter and shrugged back into it. "We aren't expecting anymore guests, are we?"

"No, they're all here," Ginny replied, forcing the pain back into its hiding place and her thoughts back to business. "You'll have to send them away. We don't have any room."

Caleb shot her another smirk. "No room in the inn, eh?"

She wrinkled her nose at him, which elicited a boisterous laugh as he thumped across the lobby, leaving wet puddles from the snow melting off his boots. She waited until the bell jingled and the door slammed closed behind him before she went to find a mop.

Ginny finished drying the floor and put her mop away in the closet off the kitchen. She returned to the lobby just as the bell jingled. Caleb's laugh soon followed, deep and reverberating in the tiny lobby. Ginny stopped in the hallway as two figures tramped in behind him and stood leaking water all over her floor. Caleb closed the door behind them and turned.

"Ah! There she is!" he exclaimed when he saw her. "This is my wife, Ginny."

"Hello," she said curtly. "I'm afraid we don't have any rooms available. Caleb." She said his name with pointed emphasis before she let her attention shift to the two guests. Immediately, she regretted her sarcasm. They were a young couple—a *very* young couple. The girl looked barely eighteen years old as she stood clutching the young man's hand, her expression contorted with worry.

Ginny felt a stab of guilt for her insensitivity. "I'm sorry," she repeated, "but we literally have no rooms left. Caleb, you know this."

The furrow between his brow deepened as she slid her gaze back to him. "I know, but she—she's—" He broke off and looked down at the floor.

Ginny glanced back at the girl just as she unbuttoned her long wool coat. It was a frayed thing with a patch on the elbow that looked like it had been stitched on by hand. Dark circles hugged the poor girl's eyes as she eased her coat open and ran a hand over her forehead, as if chasing sweat.

"Joe," she whispered, "I'm not feeling so good."

Ginny's heart constricted in her chest as she took in the girl's condition. It hadn't been visible at first, her shape hidden behind the bulky coat, but now Ginny had a very clear view of the girl's bulging abdomen. A very, very bulging abdomen.

The girl looked like she was about to explode.

Of all the places they could have stopped for help, *why* did they have to come here? An unbidden surge of jealously swept through her. It didn't seem fair that kids like this could get pregnant when they shouldn't be, when women like her who'd been waiting for years and had an established home and such deep longing couldn't seem to get pregnant no matter what they did.

She felt guilty for feeling jealous of this girl who was so clearly afraid and hurting, but the emotion was there, a cancer in her subconscious.

It was always there.

"What are you doing out on a night like this?" Ginny demanded, her voice sharper than she intended. She took a stabilizing breath before shooting a scolding look at the young man. He met her gaze head-on, fear etched in his eyes.

"We were headed to my parents' for Christmas," he said. "But we—Marian—we had to keep stopping." His voice trailed off into misery.

"It was my fault," the girl whispered. "I have to, um, stop a lot." She splayed a fragile-looking hand over her stomach. Ginny couldn't believe how rail thin the kid was; her stomach looked like a huge ball strapped onto her torso. Her bones looked too prominent, skin too thin to cover her frame.

Ginny let her eyes flicker closed. The poor girl was probably going to the bathroom like a leaky faucet. No wonder they hadn't made their destination, especially in this weather.

"It's not your fault," the boy said, his eyes flickering to Ginny and then to Caleb. "We got a late start because I got called into work last night."

"That's too bad," Caleb said. "Where do you work?"

The boy swallowed. "Taco Bell. But it's just temporary, until—until—well, we need to sort out a few things. I was going to go back to college, but with the baby…" He trailed off.

Their raw honesty about money matters and personal problems practically gave Ginny hives. She didn't want to know these details.

"I hear you," Caleb was saying. He didn't sound the least bit uncomfortable. "I hear kids can be expensive."

Ginny cleared her throat. "Why don't you sit over there by the fire?" she asked in an attempt to steer the conversation to more comfortable ground, her tone gentler than it had been before. "There's a public bathroom right off the hallway."

She was sure the girl would need it.

Marian all but collapsed into a padded antique chair right next to the blazing fire. "Do you have kids?" Her eyes were wide, intent, as if the answer were somehow vitally important.

Caleb hesitated. For the first time, his cheerful, outgoing façade flickered. He looked over his shoulder at

Ginny and held her gaze, emotions trekking across his features like a dog trampling through a flowerbed.

"No," he murmured, still watching her as he schooled his pain and tucked it away. "No, we don't."

Ginny took great care not to look at the pregnant girl sitting on her antique furniture in front of her fireplace. "I need to talk to you," she said. She worked hard to keep the wobble from her voice, but it turned to steel instead. Caleb winced, as if she'd lashed out at him. She couldn't help that. She couldn't carry his hurt as well as her own, not all the time, not now of all times.

The holidays were always the worst, when all the other families were together, celebrating with their little ones, while she and Caleb sat around an empty tree, the silence a brutal, poignant reminder of everything they didn't have. Of everything they might never have.

His boots clumped loudly as he followed her back to the kitchen. It was a large kitchen with an island in the middle with a butcher-block countertop. The cupboards were painted a dark grey, the walls a mustard yellow. Ginny stopped at the white, farmhouse-style sink and braced her palms against it.

"They can't stay here, Caleb," she said, staring out the window above the sink, at the darkness, at the plunging snow. "I can't have her here—not today—and we literally don't have any place to put them, unless you want to give up your own bed."

Her husband's silence cut like a knife. She squeezed her eyes closed, knowing she'd disappointed him yet again with her weakness, her anger, her selfish pain. It wasn't right. She shouldn't feel this way. It wasn't that girl's fault she was pregnant when Ginny wasn't, but she couldn't help it. She couldn't help how she really felt, deep down inside.

Caleb's hands settled on her shoulders, squeezing. His gentle touch brought a surge of tears to her eyes. She never understood why he loved her so much, when he was so good and kind and wholesome, and she was a cancerous lump of pain and bitterness. She didn't deserve him. She never had.

"All things happen for a reason, Ginny-girl." His voice whispered against her hair as he pressed his mouth to her dirty-blond hair. "Right now, we don't know the reasons, but we know these kids need our help. We can't turn them out. They barely made it here. The roads are becoming impassible. To send them on, to send them back out into that storm—"

"I know." Ginny sniffed. "They can stay in the lobby. I won't even charge them for the chairs."

Her poor attempt at humor earned her a gentle swat to the behind. She twisted to face him, scowling, but his half-grin and admiring eyes melted her ire.

"I love you," he said around a suppressed chuckle. "I really, really do."

She forced a frown as he kissed her forehead. "I know, but I don't understand why," she grumbled as she fished a tissue from her jeans pocket and blew her nose loudly. This was going to be a really, really bad Christmas.

"Anyway, I was thinking we could put them in the garage," Caleb continued. He rubbed the back of his neck. "At least they'd have a bed."

Ginny's eyes bugged as he referenced the makeshift apartment they had made up when renovating the B&B a few years back. "Cal, I haven't cleaned that room in ages. It's just storage."

"We've got extra blankets, haven't we? I can turn on the generator. Throw a broom around a bit."

Ginny rolled her eyes. It would take much more than that to make the room presentable, but he was right. There was a bed, and the generator would run the space heaters they hadn't needed to use since they finished renovations on the inn. She pressed a hand over her eyes and sought for another measure of strength in an already empty well.

"Fine," she conceded. "I will go find some sheets. You better get the generator running."

Ginny returned to the lobby with an armload of folded blankets and clean sheets. She pasted a fake smile on her face and tried to infuse her expression with hospitality. Why had Caleb ever thought she would make a good hostess?

"I've got good news—"

Her voice broke off as she stepped into the lobby. Marian stood next to the fire, one hand splayed against her stomach as she hunched forward, clearly in pain. Joe stood in front of her, bracing her shoulders with both hands.

"Oh, no," Ginny rasped. Her resolve evaporated as she staggered to the nearest chair and dropped her burden. Joe looked up and met her gaze across the tiny sitting area. The kid looked as if he were about to start crying at any second. "She isn't—she's not—"

"No, no, it's not the real thing," Marian whispered. "I've been having pains all week. The doctor told me they were false labor. It's too early. I'm not due for another three weeks." She hunched forward with another moan.

"They've been really bad today," Joe informed Ginny. He stared at her, pleading for help.

"How far apart are they?" Ginny asked, because it's what people always asked in the movies. She wouldn't know what to do no matter how he answered.

"I don't know—four or five minutes maybe?"

"And how long have they been going on like this?"

Joe's face blanched a little, as if he understood what she was really asking. "Since breakfast. They've been— been coming more frequently."

Ginny felt a stab of fear. That didn't sound like false labor to her. That sounded like an eighteen-year-old girl going into early labor. Her hand shook as she fished her cell phone from her back pocket. Three weeks early: how serious was that? "I'm calling nine-one-one," she announced. "We're not equipped to deal with this."

She opened up her home screen, but when she dialed, nothing happened. She stared at her phone, a chill snaking down her spine.

No signal.

How could there be no signal? Now, of all times. Yes, it happened occasionally in inclement weather, but now wasn't the time for this sort of thing to happen. Surely God knew that.

Her legs felt suddenly weak as she sank down on top of the clean linens.

Marian straightened and braced a hand against the mantle. "There, it's over. See? Nothing to worry about." Her eyes focused on her young man. "I'm fine, Joe. Truly. Girls have been doing this for centuries." Her positive tone ended in a wobble.

He managed a weak smile, but they all knew her bravado was a façade. There was definitely something to worry about here. Ginny counted the seconds until the back door slammed and Caleb's heavy footsteps announced his return. She bolted for the hallway and met him halfway.

"Is your phone working?" she all but screeched at him. "That girl is about to have a baby, and you had *better* get somebody out here right now." She punctuated her demand by jamming a finger toward the floor. By right now she meant *right now*. This second. She couldn't handle this. Even on her best day, and today was not her best day.

Christmas was the worst holiday ever.

Everyone else was celebrating the birth of a baby, but she always felt as if she were mourning the birth that would never happen. The child that would never exist.

But here there was a child making his presence known—a child that was very real, and very imminent.

And very, very early.

She twisted her hands together to hide the trembling as Caleb checked his cell phone. "Sorry," he said, sounding grim. "No reception."

"What are we going to do? That girl isn't supposed to have that baby for another *three weeks,* Caleb."

When Caleb shot a warning look toward the lobby, Ginny dropped her tone. He was right—it wouldn't do for her to lose it in front of their guests. That girl was probably freaked out enough as it was. She didn't need a loony hotel owner having a nervous breakdown while she was in the middle of contractions.

"Isn't one of the Harris party a nurse?" Caleb asked as he moved toward the lobby counter. He fished around until he found the register in the filing cabinet. She leaned over his shoulder.

"The Harris party?" she echoed, trying to remember which guests he was referring to. "The two couples from Indiana?"

"Yes! Them! The one lady said she was a nurse, I'm sure of it. What was her name? Amelia?"

Ginny cringed. She didn't remember. She tried not to get too involved in her guests' personal lives. This was a business, not a social club—something Caleb didn't seem to always understand. She envied how easily he seemed to connect with the guests, making them feel right at home even though they were complete strangers far from their normal lives and routines.

He was a natural at this hotel thing.

"They're in the Grizzly Suite," Caleb announced. "Will you go see if they're still awake? I need to get the space heaters set up."

Ginny grimaced and tried to find a good argument for them to swap places, but another moan from Marian sent her scampering toward the staircase around the corner. She took the stairs two at a time as she headed toward the suite on the south side of the B&B. All of the rooms were hunting lodge themed: the Grizzly Suite, the Wolf Suite, and so on. The Grizzly Suite sat at the end of the hallway, overlooking the thick woods and hiking trails that stretched out behind the B&B. They owned a full twenty acres, but Ginny had never explored half of it.

The day to day business kept her far too busy.

She hesitated outside the Grizzly Suite, but the faint murmur of the television gave her the courage to rap on the door. The TV muted, and then the door opened a fraction.

"I'm so sorry to bother you," Ginny rushed to say. "We have an emergency downstairs, and my husband thought someone in your group had a medical background."

The door eased closed, the chain scraping as it fell away, and then swung wide open. A man in his fifties wearing a Michigan State sweatshirt stood in the doorway, nodding to her. "My wife," he confirmed. "Hang on. She's in the bathroom. Amelia! Sweetie?" he called.

The bathroom door opened, and a woman with dark brown hair streaked with white poked her head out, a brush between her teeth. Her eyes widened, and she disappeared. The sound of running water and tapping filled the awkward silence before the woman returned. Ginny felt awful. The woman was clearly getting ready for bed, already dressed in a bathrobe and snowflake-themed fleece pajama pants.

"What is it?" she asked as she swiped a hand at her mouth as if chasing away the remnants of her toothpaste.

"We have an emergency downstairs and need help," Ginny explained. She suppressed a surge of worry. "The phones are down, and we can't call for an ambulance."

The woman's eyes turned a steely shade of gray as she shrugged out of her bathrobe and into a pair of tennis shoes. She laced them up quickly and hurried into the hall. "What's going on?"

Ginny led her down the hall to the stairs, explaining in a rush about the young couple and the worrisome contractions. "We're setting up a room in the garage, but I'm afraid it's no place for a woman in her condition. She needs to go to the hospital."

Amelia Harris glanced out the large bay windows as they rounded the corner to the lobby. "That's probably not going to happen," she said grimly.

Ginny froze when she found the lobby empty. "They must already be in the garage. You're going to need a coat." She pulled her good coat from the closet and handed it to the woman before shrugging into a thin canvas jacket she usually wore in the autumn months.

They hurried into the kitchens and out the back door. The air immediately bit into her, the snow thick and heavy as it created a barrier between them and the faint glow of lights from the garage's exterior light. It was set back a ways from the inn, closer to the forest. Through the heavy snowfall, she couldn't even see the building.

"Sorry, it's going to be a short walk," Ginny huffed as she hunched into her thin coat and headed toward the faint glow of light. "I should have just given them our room."

Amelia's laugh mingled with heavy breathing as she fell into step beside Ginny. "Hindsight," she joked. "Always a day late."

The garage light grew brighter as they approached. Ginny shouldered the door open. It always stuck, and she had to heave twice before she got it to swing open. She kicked it hard to close it, mumbling an apology at her guest. "Dumb door," she muttered.

The garage was cluttered with odds and ends for the day to day upkeep of the B&B. They wove through the racks and tables until they reached the wooden staircase at the back. The stairs led up to a single room apartment. It only had the basics, bathroom and running water. They'd moved the stove and fridge to the main building once repairs had been completed.

Ginny found Marian pacing while the two men tried to put clean sheets on the bed. She stooped to gather up the plastic covering they'd discarded and set it off to one side before stepping up to Joe in order to take over. "Let me," she said. She quickly strapped the fitted sheet around the corner of the mattress.

"Wait a minute," Amelia called. "You may want to put the plastic underneath the sheets."

Ginny froze as she considered what the woman was saying. The only reason to put the plastic back on was to protect the mattress, and that meant Amelia expected they might be getting things messy.

Did she seriously expect them to deliver a baby? Here? Tonight?

Mouth dry, she did as instructed, exchanging worried looks with Caleb as Amelia began speaking calmly to the young couple. "How far apart on the contractions? Are you timing them?"

"It's just false labor," Marian answered, one hand against the small of her back. "It's too early."

Amelia's gaze shifted to the young man.

Joe's voice sounded strained when he replied. "I, uh, have an app on my phone, but I haven't tried using it yet."

"Time to learn how," the nurse said with a cheerful smile. "This has been going on all day?"

Joe nodded as he fished his phone from his back pocket.

"Well, let's start timing a few, and then maybe I'll check you, see if you're dilating yet."

Ginny straightened as they finished making the bed. "What kind of nurse are you?"

"Don't worry," Amelia said, turning toward her with a calm smile. "I've helped deliver dozens of babies. I've never done it on my own, but the process is very natural. We just help it along a little."

A huge weight lifted from Ginny's shoulders, knowing the burden would no longer be hers to carry. She could get the room straightened up and get out of here as soon as possible. She shoved a few boxes to the side and took the broom from Caleb so she could sweep away months of dust and discarded debris left by mice and squirrels. The room was already beginning to warm from the three space heaters Caleb had distributed around.

"That one was three minutes," Amelia's cheerful voice said. "Things might be progressing here, my dear. What's your name again?"

"Marian," the poor girl moaned. "The baby can't be coming. I'm not—I'm not ready yet!"

Amelia laughed and patted her on the back. "Don't worry. Let's time a few more, and then I'll check you out." Her eyes shifted across the room to Ginny. "I'm going to need a few things."

Ginny nodded and swallowed the lump that still clogged the back of her throat. Amelia showed Joe how to keep timing the contractions, instructing Marian to keep walking about, if she could. She came over to join Ginny near the doorway. "We're going to need boiling water, clean towels, rubbing alcohol, soap, plastic gloves if you have them."

When another moan echoed through the garage apartment, Amelia's mouth set in a firmer line. "And probably coffee. I think we're going to need it."

"So she's really having the baby? Now?" Ginny forced the words past stiff lips, wondering when she could escape and leave this nightmare for someone else to deal with.

Amelia just shrugged. "It's hard to say," she confessed. "Babies are unpredictable. I'll need to perform a pelvic exam to see how far she's dilated." Her eyes lingered on Ginny, as if searching for something. "I could use a hand, if you're feeling up to it. To keep Daddy calm, if nothing else."

Ginny found herself nodding even though everything in her screamed that she run in the other direction.

It seemed her worst fears were coming true: this was going to be the worst Christmas.

Ever.

CHAPTER TWO

CALEB JOINED GINNY in the kitchen while she waited for the pot of water to boil. She huddled beside the stove, arms wrapped around herself, and looked up miserably when he clattered into the house from outside. A draft of frigid air curled around her and made her sink deeper into herself.

He paused on the mat and removed his gloves, his eyes searching hers. "Aw, babe," he finally said. Tears filled her eyes unbidden as he crossed the small space to reach her. She buried her face in the cold fabric of his winter parka and let her tears soak into him. She imagined the pain leaking out of her and leeching into him, and this made her cry even harder.

He was so good to her.

"I'm sorry," she cried as his arms tightened around her, his chin resting on the top of her head. "I'm trying to be strong, I really am, but this is so hard. Why does it have to be so hard?"

"I know," he whispered, his voice husky and rough. Now she really hated herself, because she was reminding him of his own secret pains.

They just wanted a child—just one precious little child to call their own. Was that so much to ask? Why had God chosen them out of all the couples in the world to be another Hannah and What's-his-name? It didn't seem fair. They would make great parents. They were well-situated, loving people; no child of theirs would ever be abused or go hungry.

Why would God put children into homes like that when He wouldn't put one into theirs?

"We can't force it to happen if it isn't meant to be," Caleb finally said. His quiet words cut like daggers into her soul.

She squeezed her eyes closed. Was he giving up? Had he finally lost hope, after all these years of trying? Of special diets and research? Ovulation tests? Consultations with doctors? Period after period of reminders that she wasn't pregnant, that they'd failed yet again, over and over again…

Were all those tears for nothing? Just salty water to fill up a well of pain that would never be emptied?

She sobbed harder. Now she was being melodramatic.

"I wish I could tell you to just go to bed and not worry about any of this," he said at long length, his arms squeezing a little tighter. "But there's a girl out there who needs us—who needs you. They're ready for the supplies. They need you, love. I know it doesn't help, and I know it isn't fair, but they need you."

Ginny pulled back and sniffed loudly, wiping her nose with the back of her hand. She looked at the drainage on her hand and groaned and flapped it around while she hunted for a box of tissues. After blowing her nose, she scrubbed her hands in the sink until her skin burned, trying to wash away the pain while she prepared herself for what had to be done.

She tried to picture Marian's face, pinched and pale and framed with limp blond hair. She was so young and probably so scared. She inhaled raggedly and stared out the window, at the snow that only seemed to fall heavier and heavier, burying her beneath the weight of the coldness inside her.

"I'm ready," she finally said as she turned away from her own wobbling reflection in the dark glass. The water had begun to boil on the stove, so Caleb put the lid on it and grabbed it with gloved hands while Ginny picked up the large metal bowl she used for canning peaches filled with the items Amelia had listed, as well as a small first aid kit, scissors, the box of tissues Ginny had just found, and anything else she could think of that they might need.

"I feel like Laura Ingalls Wilder," she muttered. "What is this, the Stone Age?"

Caleb laughed as he followed her to the door and out into the snow. The wind blew with a faint whistle, driving damp snow into her as she battled her way toward the glow from the garage. "I hear people do this at home all the time," he said, tramping alongside her, his breath white against the air.

"Where do you hear that?" Ginny shot back. She sounded annoyed, but they both knew she wasn't mad him. She was coping, the only way she knew how. She often wished she could be one of those perpetually sweet and happy people, but the truth of the matter was, she wasn't like that. She was sarcastic and impatient and felt things too keenly to hide it sometimes.

She may be walking in Hannah's shoes, but she certainly didn't have her grace or temperament.

Maybe God was punishing her for that, for not being the better person.

As Caleb kicked the garage door open, she winced and scolded herself. She knew that wasn't true. She knew God didn't punish folks just to be cruel, to prove some Providential point. Her life was just part of the plan, that was all. Part of some big plan she didn't understand.

A muted wail from above halted her at the foot of the stairs while Caleb thundered up a little faster. Why couldn't she be more like him? Running toward the pain rather than trying to hide from it? She forced her wooden legs to mount the steps, one at a time, over and over again until she turned at the top landing and stepped into the dusty apartment. Heat radiated from within now that the space heaters had been doing their work for a while. Outside, the winter storm continued to rage a battle that seemed in tune to the screaming of her own heart.

Marian leaned forward, gripping the footboard of the bed while Joe rubbed her back in quick, frantic circles.

"Can't you do anything to help her? To make it go faster?" he asked Amelia.

The nurse shook her head and smiled grimly at him. "I'm sorry, but nature must take its course. She'll pull through. But I won't lie to you, it's going to be hard. She needs you to be strong. For her. For the baby."

Ginny felt as if the stranger was speaking to her where she lurked in the doorway, afraid to come any closer. How was it her words were timed so perfectly for Ginny's arrival?

How was it she even happened to be here? What were the chances that a nurse would be at their bed and breakfast this weekend? And not just any nurse, but one who actually knew how to deliver babies. Ginny was sure they didn't all know how to do that.

Maybe God really did have this all planned out. Now she just had to do her part.

She stepped across the room with short, jerky steps and set her supplies down on a faded carboard box of unused Christmas decorations. Caleb always went overboard with the holiday decorating, and they always had more baubles and strands of garland than the walls had space for.

"I think I got it all," Ginny informed Amelia. Her voice sounded small, pathetic.

Amelia looked up from where she was monitoring Marian's pulse. "Great. I want to check her. I think things are moving along." She glanced at Caleb suddenly. "We may want something to cover the floor—a tarp? Trash bags? Take your time, so we can have some privacy. After that, we probably won't need you for a while."

Her bluntness somehow made Ginny feel better about the situation. She wanted Caleb here with her but realized all too well that Marian didn't need some strange man in the room when she was in this state.

Caleb gave her a quick peck on the cheek before he lumbered out the door. His footsteps faded into silence.

"All right, girl, let's get you into the bed. I need you take everything off from the waist down. Baby Daddy will help you—husband? Boyfriend?"

Ginny felt a twinge of guilt that she hadn't thought to get more information from them when they'd first met.

"Boyfriend," Joe whispered, sounding miserable. "We didn't mean to get pregnant, and we want to get married, but we couldn't afford it, not with needing to get ready for the baby and all. We didn't even know she was pregnant until she started gaining weight. She's always been, you know, irregular." His cheeks turned bright pink as he discussed the womanly things girls didn't think twice about.

"Don't you worry about that," Amelia told him, sounding firm. "It'll all come together. The important thing is that you're here for her and you do right by her. Now, you get her situated and we'll wait over here until you're ready for us."

Ginny hurriedly joined her along the wall and peered intently through the single window in the apartment as she tried to ignore the moans from behind them.

"It hurts so bad," Marian whispered, clearly for Joe's ears alone. "I never thought it could hurt so bad."

"I'm sorry, real sorry, Mare," he whispered back. "I never knew—I mean—I never thought—I didn't mean for this to happen."

There was a moment of silence and then Marian sniffled. "Are you disappointed? I know this isn't what we planned. What we wanted."

"Disappointed? Heck, no!" His voice rose a bit.

Amelia and Ginny exchanged glances, her expression mirroring what Ginny felt in her soul. She felt *sorry* for these kids, two foolish kids who'd gotten themselves into a tight spot and were now facing the realities of life. As much as she wanted a baby, she wouldn't have wanted one under these circumstances.

For the first time since they'd arrived, Ginny allowed herself to contemplate the idea a child wasn't the cure-all for her problems. Yes, she wanted one more than breath in her lungs, but did that mean being a parent would be easy? Did it mean that not having a child when she was an eighteen-year-old kid, scared out of her mind, was a bad thing? Could she have done what Marian was being forced to do right this moment?

Ginny inhaled a ragged breath, acknowledging for the first time in many months, perhaps many years, that she was glad there was a plan and that she didn't have complete control of it.

Amelia reached over and squeezed her arm. "Best thing you can do for them is be strong," she murmured, her voice barely audible and clearly intended for Ginny alone. "Stay calm, no matter what happens. All right?"

She nodded. She may not like it, she didn't have to, but she could do this.

CHAPTER THREE

THE NIGHT PASSED in a blur of repetition. Ginny had never realized how long labor could be, how short the breaks were in between contractions, how intense the agony of bringing life into the world was. She'd never seen such pain, such exhaustion, on anyone the way she saw it etched on Marian's young face. As night crept toward dawn, she could tell Amelia was beginning to worry.

Marian's cries had turned to screams. The time for waiting out contractions had passed, and now she was pushing, again and again, but the baby didn't want to come.

Marian fell back after a wave had passed, gasping and crying. Joe huddled beside her, trying to hold her as best he could in the awkward way they had her propped with sweat-soaked pillows. Amelia and Ginny hunched at the foot of the bed, trying to help the poor girl get into position as each contraction began. Amelia glanced at Ginny, sweat soaking her forehead, her hair frizzing around her hairline.

"She's getting tired," she breathed, careful to keep her gloved hands away from her body to avoid contaminating them. Ginny'd been trying hard to mimic her movements, doing everything she could to keep cool cloths on Marian's face and neck, water for her to sip.

Poor Joe hadn't had anything to drink in hours. He refused to leave Marian's side for a second. There was terror in his eyes, real terror.

Ginny wondered what was worse: feeling the pain or watching the one you loved most in the world go through it and having no power at all to help them?

"Is she going to be okay?" she asked, her voice as hushed as Amelia's.

She smiled, but it looked strained, forced. "This baby needs to come," she finally replied. "If we were in a hospital…well, I don't doubt the doctors would be discussing a cesarean by now. She's been pushing too long."

"It's coming again," Marian cried, her body tensing as she pushed up on her hands, her body straining with the pain.

"Don't fight the contractions," Amelia ordered. "I need you to push, Marian. Push."

Marian's cry turned guttural as she pushed through the contraction until she collapsed weakly against the pillows, gasping incoherent words.

Ginny closed her eyes, a slow tremble sweeping through her body. *Please, God,* she begged. *Don't let it end like this, her in such pain, the baby…don't let her lose it. Don't let him lose* them. *Bring this babe into the world. For them. For them. God, please, give it to them. I don't care if I never have a child: if has to be this way, give the child to her. Please, fix this.*

Her silent cries for mercy dissipated as Marian rose up with another contraction. They were coming so fast and hard now, barely giving her respite between waves.

Another. And another.

Joe was near frantic, his eyes glassy when he looked up, begging them silently do something. To do anything.

"I can see the head now," Amelia called. "Marian, I can see the head. Here, give me your hand. Can you feel it?" She grabbed Marian's trembling fingers and pulled them into position. Fear and agony filled the poor girl's expression, but as her fingers brushed the child she fought so hard to bring into the world, something else crept into her eyes.

Determination.

She wasn't done fighting yet.

"That's a good girl," Ginny murmured as she brought a fresh cloth to wipe Marian's face. "You've got this. Your baby's coming. He's coming now. You can do this. Just a few more pushes."

Her eyes met Ginny's briefly. When Ginny grabbed her fingers, Marian squeezed hard, her body too exhausted, too focused, to communicate with words.

Another contraction pulled her attention away, back to the child who needed her.

"That's good, Marian! The biggest push you can imagine, do it now!" Amelia called.

Marian's fingers dug into Ginny's hand, biting, but she let the girl squeeze the life from her hand and willed that life into the baby.

"He's coming!" Amelia cried. "Marian, I've got him. You've done it."

The girl fell back with a choking sob, her fingers still clinging to Ginny's. Joe stroked her face, his forehead pressed to hers. "You've done it, Mare, you've done it." He sounded as if he was crying.

A frail cry filled the garage, the sound of life, beautiful and agonizing at once.

Ginny realized she was crying too and shifted her shoulder to wipe tears away. Amelia appeared with a bloody, soiled towel, and Ginny moved the side as the nurse in her snowflake pajamas placed the bundle in Marian's waiting arms.

"It's a boy," Amelia announced with a grin, over the wails of the baby. "With a nice set of lungs."

Joe's face turned a sickly shade of white. "A boy. Wow. A son. I'm a—I'm a dad."

"You're going to be awesome," Marian whispered. "We're going to be okay. All of us. We're going to be okay."

She began to cry as he pressed his forehead to hers again and stretched a tentative arm out to include the tiny bundle in her arms.

Ginny turned away to compose herself as Amelia began to work on Marian again. It seemed the battle wasn't over quite yet. Amelia began to talk about things like afterbirth and the placenta, details which honestly made Ginny's stomach churn. She stayed out of the way, handing Amelia clean towels when she needed them and discarding the soiled ones, trying not to watch what was happening.

At last, Amelia stripped off her gloves and glanced over at Ginny, a tired smile turning her lips. "I think you can take a break now," she said with a slight laugh. "You look like you need it."

"I'll go get us more coffee," she suggested, grateful for the excuse to escape the garage and sort out her jumbled emotions.

Amelia's eyes brightened. "And I'm sure I look like I need *that*," she joked.

Ginny found herself laughing as she left to wash her hands in the bathroom before slipping into the bulky hunting coat Caleb had left for her instead of the canvas jacket. She stepped out of the garage into a murky dawn. The snow was still falling, but it seemed to be slowing down. Caleb had shoveled a path to the inn, although an inch had accumulated since he'd last been out. Ginny found him in the kitchen, asleep at the table with Amelia's husband snoring in a rocker nearby.

Evidence of how they'd entertained themselves throughout the night cluttered her kitchen. Sandwich fixings sat on the countertop beside two empty plates. A pot half full of popcorn sat on the stove, the jar of kernels left open to one side, the coconut oil sitting beside it without a lid. Candy wrappers littered the table, mingled with a scattered deck of Uno cards.

She rolled her eyes. Twelve years of marriage, and Caleb still hadn't learned how to pick up after himself.

She punched Caleb's arm to wake him up. He bolted upright, hair tousled and eyes bleary with sleep. When he focused on her, he sat up a little straighter. "Is it over?" he asked, sounding anxious.

Ginny's irritation over the state of her kitchen dissipated. She nodded and sank into the chair beside him. "Yes," she said. "It's over. A boy. They both seem okay."

Caleb smiled and folded his hand over hers, his fingers hot and comforting and familiar, as familiar as her own hands. She leaned over to kiss his knuckles, so thankful he was a part of her life. Who else in this world would put up with her the way he did?

"How are you?" he asked. She lifted her head and met his gaze. His pale eyes searched hers, unspoken questions in their depths.

Ginny wasn't sure at first. She tried to sort out her feelings, but they were so jumbled together she couldn't tell where sorrow began and exhilaration ended. Everything was a muddle. But maybe that was the way it was supposed to be, a little of both, not too much of either.

"I'm okay," she said at last, squeezing his hand. She smiled at him past the exhaustion. "Caleb, I'm okay."

For the first time in a long while, she truly meant it.

Marian smiled as Ginny crept into apartment with Caleb behind her. Amelia had done a great job of cleaning up the room; even the trash bags on the floor had been gathered up and bagged. Ginny felt that sense of panic as she saw the young girl holding the precious bundle in her arms. The blanket moved, a weak mewl announcing the child's presence.

As if Ginny needed the reminder.

"We, uh, we just wanted to make sure you had everything you need," she managed weakly from where she had planted herself right inside the doorway. She had no intention of stepping a foot further into the room.

Joe grinned at them from where he perched alongside Marian and the baby. "You gotta come see him!" he called. "He's great—and so strong already. Look! He's holding my finger!"

Caleb's hand found her elbow and squeezed. She wanted to weep and run from the room. It was bad enough she'd been forced to endure this traumatic ordeal, but asking her to pretend like she was happy when she was so miserable…

It wasn't that she was angry at the baby, or at Marian and Caleb. She was happy for them—she *wanted* to be happy for them, but just now her emotions were so raw, that tiny little bundle of joy too poignant a reminder of what she didn't have.

Of what she might never have.

Caleb's hand nudged her forward. She resisted the urge to scowl at him. How could he be so calm? She knew this had to bother him as much as it did her, but he was so stinking good at hiding his feelings. Nobody would ever suspect for a minute that he wasn't as content and happy as he pretended to be.

Caleb finally left her in the doorway, walking away without her. She felt a chill snake up her spine as he abandoned her so he could go play happy host. He was so good at everything that it made her feel so rotten.

She remembered her frantic prayers from earlier, that God spare Marian and the baby no matter what happened in Ginny's own life. Another shard of guilt stabbed her.

Had she really meant that? If she did mean it, then she should be walking across this dirty floor right now, congratulating Marian and Joe and cooing over their precious gift.

If she didn't, well, then she'd stay where she was, hiding on the fringes of the room.

"Well, now, he sure is a strapping boy."

Caleb's words dug into her thoughts and yanked her back to the present. She saw him sitting on a cardboard box, his bulky arms curved to hold Marian's baby. Tears sprang into Ginny's eyes as she watched him, so capable, so tender. If given half a chance, he would make an incredible father.

"Ginny, you need to come see this! I think he's looking at me!" Caleb looked up at her, wonder filling his face, pleading in his eyes. He stared across the apartment and waited.

He expected her to perform her duty, to be hospitable and gracious. This is what they did.

She forced her legs to move and pasted a smile on her frozen lips. Marian beamed at her as she approached the bed and the box where Caleb sat. The baby blinked tiredly, eyes unfocused but dark and compelling. She doubted the boy could see much yet, but it did seem like he tried to focus on her as she stopped beside Caleb.

"He's very cute," she said. It wasn't entirely true. The baby's skin was mottled red, purple, and pasty white. He had a head of hair on him though, dark strands still damp from his cozy home inside his mother.

"Here, you need to hold him," Caleb said. He was voice was husky as he rose slowly from the box.

Ginny took a frantic step backward: that was asking too much. "I—I can't!" she sputtered.

But Caleb stood there and waited until she sank onto the box and he eased the child into her arms. He was so light, so fragile, she feared she would break him if she squeezed even a little. He whimpered slightly before settling in. His tiny eyelids began to flutter and droop.

"He's tired from his big workout," Amelia said with a chuckle. "It's not easy being born."

Marian managed a breathless laugh. "You can say that again."

"But it was worth it!" Joe exclaimed. "I mean, wasn't it?"

Ginny tore her eyes away from the baby to see Marian reach out and take Joe's hand in hers. She looked exhausted, covered in sweat, but still she smiled. "Yeah, it was worth it. Totally worth it."

Ginny looked back down at the baby as Caleb knelt beside her, one arm reaching around her waist as his other hand tweaked the blanket just slightly so he could have a better view of the boy's face. She'd been wrong about one thing. She and Caleb might be more financially sound to raise a baby, but this one would be no less loved by his parents.

They were clearly smitten.

Who was she to say if their home would have been a better choice?

"You're going to have a good life," she whispered to the baby and began to rock him gently side to side. "You've got an amazing mommy and daddy, little man. They're going to take good care of you."

She turned toward Caleb, tears in her eyes, but that was okay. In this moment, she was truly happy for these two kids and the precious package they'd been willing to share with her, for just a few moments. She rested her cheek against Caleb's shoulder, his embrace tightening as if he understood.

It was a bittersweet moment, full of joy and regret, hope and loss.

But that was okay too. At least they were going through it together. No matter what happened, they had that.

CHAPTER FOUR

CALEB FINALLY GOT through to nine-one-one. Ginny felt no small measure of pride when she overheard him telling the dispatcher that he didn't think there was any immediate danger, that the nurse and his wife had taken care of everything.

The paramedics arrived before Caleb managed to get the driveway shoveled, but after the road plow had made one pass. Joe and Amelia's husband ran out to help him finish clearing enough of the driveway to get the ambulance closer to the garage while the paramedics went up to check on Marian and the baby.

Ginny rose to let the paramedics take her place, but Marian grabbed her hand. She froze and glanced down at the young girl, barely into womanhood and already a mother. She looked exhausted, but the agony had vanished from her expression. "Thank you," she said. "We can never repay you."

Ginny squeezed her fingers and leaned over to tuck the blanket in around her wee one, filled with so many bittersweet emotions. "No payment necessary," she told her with a wry grin. "It's Christmas after all."

A smile blossomed on Marian's face. "He's a Christmas baby, isn't he?" Her smile wobbled suddenly. "Do you think he'll like that? I mean, he's gonna get all his presents on one day." The concerned look on her face let Ginny know she was entirely in earnest.

The thought would never have crossed her mind. She felt a pang as she realized Marian's motherly instincts were already kicking in, that need to shelter, to protect, to love.

"Well," Ginny began slowly. "Jesus doesn't seem to mind it, does he?"

Marian looked thoughtful for a moment. "Good point. What do you think we should name him?"

She stilled. No one had ever asked her that question before. What would be a good name for a Christmas baby? Finally, she just laughed and shook her head. "I don't know. I think you should name him what *you* want. Might want to give Joe a vote, though."

Marian giggled, and the sound reminded Ginny of Christmas bells tinkling on the tree.

Caleb and Ginny stood on the front porch, arms linked as the ambulance eased out of the driveway, tires spinning over the snow as it battled for traction. Amelia went inside to shower and probably go to bed. For some reason, they lingered outside in the cold even as the taillights disappeared into the early morning.

"Seems we had our own little Nativity story going on this weekend," Caleb said.

"What do you mean?"

"Joe? Marian? A baby? No room in the inn?"

"Don't be silly," Ginny scoffed. "You don't—you don't suppose—"

"What? That God sent them here for a reason? Of course, I think that. And you do too, or you will, when you've thought about it for half a second."

She slugged him on the arm. Caleb grinned and snugged her a little closer as he kissed the top of her head. "I really am proud of you, you know."

Ginny reveled in the warmth his words brought, a little proud of herself as well. "I feel like I was hit by a bulldozer," she said instead, twisting to give him a wry smile.

He chuckled and kissed the tip of her nose. "You would say that."

"I would," she agreed with another cheeky smile.

He snaked both arms around her, and she turned to lose herself in his embrace. The strength of his arms was just what she needed this morning—this Christmas morning.

She groaned. "I need to start breakfast. It's going to be late. Hope no one will mind."

"I'm sure they won't, under the circumstances," he consoled her. His chest vibrated with suppressed laughter.

"What?" she demanded, pulling back. "Are you *laughing* at me?"

Caleb broke out in a full laugh. "I love you," he said, grinning as he kissed first one cheek and then the other.

"I should say I love you too, but right now I'm more inclined to make *you* go do breakfast," she grumbled playfully.

He stared down into her eyes, his dimples deep and familiar. "I don't suppose we could celebrate a bit later this morning—after breakfast of course." His lips twitched, eyes filled with promises of mischief and more celebration than eggnog and Christmas carols.

Ginny pursed her lips. "I'm sure I don't know what you mean," she said, but she leaned up on her toes and kissed him. When he deepened their kiss, she began to wonder if breakfast could possibly wait.

But just then the door jangled behind them. Ginny ripped away from him, mortified as she smoothed her hair. Amelia's husband stood in the doorway, smirking at them.

"Sorry to interrupt," he said, flicking merry eyes between her and Caleb, "but we don't seem to have any hot water."

Ginny groaned as real life returned with a resounding *thwump* of responsibilities. "Of course, we don't," she muttered. She shot Caleb a knowing look. "You better go take care of that while I do breakfast."

Amelia's husband disappeared back inside. Caleb backed away, grinning at her. *Later*, he mouthed with a wink before he too went inside and left her alone on the porch. Ginny hesitated, knowing breakfast wouldn't make itself, but she took a moment to enjoy the quiet, the pristine white of the heavy snowdrifts.

It was going to be a beautiful Christmas.

EPILOGUE

Three weeks later…

GINNY LOWERED THE toilet seat lid and sat down, her stomach churning with all-too-familiar insecurities and doubts.

Her period was almost five days late.

But this wasn't that abnormal, she told herself. It happened occasionally. And it seemed like every time it happened, she took a pregnancy test and then started her period later that day. It was like a cruel joke. She'd stopped taking pregnancy tests about a year ago, simply riding out the wait until nature took its course.

This morning she'd found an unused pregnancy test in the back of the cabinet. It had probably fallen out of the box the last time she used them. She held the package in her hand, debating with herself. She could just throw it away. Might be easier than suffering the disappointment of another negative result.

She could do that.

But her thoughts flickered back to the events of Christmas Day. What had begun as a day out of her worst nightmares had somehow turned into something beautiful. No, it still hadn't been easy, but she'd survived and come out better for it at the other end.

So, yes, she could just throw away the unused test and continue with her life the way she had been these last few months, burying her hopes deep inside where no one could see them.

Caleb's heavy footsteps thudded down the hall as he prepared to go out and snow blow the drive—Ginny had finally consented and let him buy one during the post-Christmas sales. He whistled a Christmas carol as he walked—and would be for the next six months until she threatened to stop feeding him if he didn't do away with the caroling until Thanksgiving.

The words to *Mary, Did You Know* sprang unbidden into her mind. It was a beautiful song, melancholy and gripping, and filled her with a sort of sadness. Maybe she should just throw away the test. It was easier than clinging to a pointless hope.

Caleb burst into song, somewhere in the lobby. His deep bass, mildly off-key but no less enthusiastic, echoed down the hall to where she cowered in the bathroom.

For some reason, Joe and Marian sprang into her thoughts. They'd received a letter earlier in the week with a picture of little Tyler Immanuel and an invitation to their wedding later in the spring. Ginny had already RSVP'd. Somehow, it felt like the right thing to do.

She still couldn't believe how the events of that night had unfolded. It almost seemed too uncanny, Caleb's modern-day Nativity scenario. Even Ginny couldn't deny the unusual parallels.

God had a sense of humor, that was for sure.

The package crinkled in her hands as she looked down at the unopened pregnancy test. In a burst of confidence, she ripped it open and slid the white tube with the pink cap out of the plastic wrap.

Yes, God did have a sense of humor, but He was also loving and caring and busy planning out her life. She didn't know what the future held for her, for Caleb, for the child they wanted so badly but feared they would never have. But she wasn't ready to give up hope.

So she stood, lifted the toilet seat, then removed the cap from the test strip. Until God told her otherwise, she was going to keep on hoping.

Maybe the time for waiting was finally over.

THE END

SNEAK PEEK
FROM *THE CARPENTER'S WIFE*

PROLOGUE

July 2019

GINNY LATHAM CROSSED her arms as her husband, Caleb, downed an entire glass of lemonade in one long gulp. He grinned at her beneath the shade of the wraparound porch of the Timeless Bed & Breakfast. The inn was their pride and joy and a perpetual headache of repairs. She took the glass he offered her.

"*Now* can we discuss the hinges on the back door?" she asked with a playful pout. "Again?" She laughed to pretend she wasn't really mad.

She had only asked him to replace the rusted hinges three times. The squeaking got on her nerves, and WD-40 did nothing to help.

Caleb sighed and wiped sweat from his forehead. "I'll do it now." His gaze flitted away as a white jeep slowed down in front of the Timeless driveway, and the driver slid a handful of envelopes into the mailbox. "I'll grab the mail and get right on it."

She huffed under her breath as he strolled from the porch and down the long drive. "I'll believe that when I see it!" she called after him, unable to resist.

He threw a grin over his shoulder as if her irritation and nagging didn't bother him. Which, based on how long it was taking him to fix her hinges, suggested he truly wasn't bothered. She couldn't help but admire the way his broad shoulders moved as he walked and how the sun enhanced the natural highlights in his auburn hair. He stopped to admire one of the flowerbeds before continuing his meander to the mailbox.

He was taking his time on purpose.

He always stopped to smell the roses. She meant that figuratively and literally, and it drove her absolutely batty. No wonder it took him three weeks to change out a couple of hinges when he had to stop and admire every flower in the blooming state of Michigan.

Caleb began to whistle as he opened the mailbox and pulled out the stack of envelopes. There seemed to be a lot of them. She hoped most of it was advertisements and not bills. Some days she felt like all she did was keep track of expenses. Not that they were struggling, but in this economy one couldn't take anything for granted.

Her husband's whistling broke off abruptly. Ginny watched as he tucked the mail under his arm and began yanking twigs out of the mailbox with more fervor than seemed entirely necessary. His good mood seemed dampened as he tossed the twigs onto the ground, muttering to himself. From a nearby maple tree, a bird twittered wrathfully.

Ginny couldn't help but smirk.

One of the joys of living in the middle of nowhere was dealing with the wildlife that also enjoyed the solitude, and Caleb had been enjoying a stubborn bird for nearly a week. The stupid thing had decided their mailbox would make a great nest, no matter how many times Caleb emptied her hard work all over the street.

Honestly, Ginny felt sorry for the bird. If she were

expecting, she wouldn't want some auburn-haired giant upending her nursery every morning.

Ginny would put up with almost anything, including auburn-haired giants and nursery demolition, if it meant she might have a child of her own. If *they* might have a child of *their* own. She knew Caleb wanted it as badly as she did. Even though it hurt, she still kept a large supply of pregnancy tests in her bathroom, just in case. She hadn't given up hope that a child may be waiting in their future.

Caleb slammed the mailbox shut with a satisfied jerk of his chin and headed toward her, a bit more pep in his stride. He looked rather cute when he was irritated.

She wondered if he thought the same thing about her and if that was why he never rushed through her lengthy to-do lists.

"We've got a letter from the Carpenters," he announced, waving a rectangular envelope. "Probably their Thank Yous."

Ginny accepted the envelope and murmured her agreement. Joe and Marian Carpenter had invited them to their wedding back in May, and although they really didn't know the young couple well, Ginny had felt obligated to go after the events last Christmas. The birth of little Tyler in the inn's garage had certainly created a stir at Timeless. She was glad they'd decided to attend, despite her reservations; the wedding was small, only around fifty guests, and the young couple had seemed thrilled at their attendance.

She slid her finger along the flap and tugged a single sheet of lined paper from the envelope. When she shot a wry look at Caleb, he grinned at her.

"It doesn't matter if they bought a five-dollar Thank You card or a dollar pad of paper." He sounded as if he were admonishing her. "It's the sentiment that matters, Ginny-love."

"I didn't say anything." Although she protested in her

own defense, her cheeks heated. He'd guessed right; her thoughts had immediately noticed the lack of a proper thank you card.

The letter filled nearly a page. She sat down in a nearby rocker to read it out loud. It was filled with the usual effusive thanks for their generous monetary gift and the pleasure of their attendance. The second half of the letter, however, contained personal updates on the family. Little Tyler was under weight for his age but seemed happy. Joe still worked at Taco Bell but hoped something more promising would open up soon. They had moved out of their friend's basement and into an apartment of their own.

"Nothing in there about Marian?" Caleb asked when she finished, intuitive as always.

Ginny studied the girl's graceful signature with a mild frown. She hadn't noticed that. "She's probably wrapped up in her new role as wife and mother." But her fingers smoothed the wrinkled paper as she skimmed through the letter a second time, wondering how the teenage girl was truly faring.

Maybe she should give her a call sometime.

But who was she fooling? Ginny'd think about calling, feel guilty for not calling, but in the end her hatred of phones and natural introvert instincts would win over, and the call would remain unplaced for weeks. Perhaps months.

Sometimes you just couldn't change who you were.

CHAPTER ONE

Five months later…

LATE NOVEMBER RAIN pummeled the windowpanes as Marian Carpenter sat in her second-hand glider, a feverish Tyler Immanuel sleeping restlessly against her neck. This time of year in southern Michigan, the weather proved so unpredictable: one day there could be rain flooding their basement apartment, and the next snow could be a foot deep outside their patio door. She tucked the blanket a little closer around the babe as he whimpered and resettled himself. Thunder crackled in the distance, ominous, like the growl of an angry bear. Marian shifted the rocker with the toe of one tattered tennis shoe, careful to rock only a little so that the cranky old glider wouldn't screech in protest and wake Tyler.

He was going to be one in about a month. One year old already. How had this year flown by so quickly? It seemed like just yesterday they got stuck in a snowbank outside the Timeless Bed & Breakfast Inn. How fortuitous that had been.

If it hadn't been for Caleb and Ginny Latham, the middle-aged couple who owned the inn, Marian might have given birth in that dratted snowbank with only her panicky and clueless Joe for a doctor.

She rocked too far, and the chair shrieked in protest.

Drat the crotchety old thing.

She froze as Tye sighed against her neck, his breath hot. She shouldn't complain; Joe had found the glider on the side of the road, tossed out by its previous owner who'd probably gotten sick of the squeaking. It had been missing the seat cushion, but Marian was able to make a replacement out of an old couch pillow they'd found at Goodwill. It didn't fit quite right and was lumpy, but it was better than nothing.

Beggars couldn't be choosers, as the saying went.

They might not be sitting at the intersection outside the mall begging for pennies, but they were probably as close to beggars as anyone could come. Even though she and Joe had both turned eighteen recently, she didn't feel like she'd grown up. Adulthood felt elusive and terrifying. She pursed her lips and tried to ignore the perpetual ache of worry in her stomach as she thought about their empty bank account and the pile of bills on the table. The electric bill was still past due, but at least they'd been able to scrape enough together to pay rent on time this month. Their landlord was as patient as she could be, all things considered, but even kindly old Mrs. Grace expected to get paid eventually. She was already doing them a favor by renting out her studio apartment for a pittance.

Joe and Marian could never have afforded anything else, not on the paychecks Joe brought home from Taco Bell. That job was supposed to be temporary, but the months crawled by and nothing else presented itself. Joe was young, inexperienced, without a college education…there weren't many opportunities available to him. Marian ached for him; he deserved a chance. She could see his good qualities and wished someone else would as well.

Thunder rumbled again. Marian glanced at the stove to check the time. Almost midnight. Joe was an hour late. If he was working late, he usually used the store phone to call and let her know. They could only afford one track phone, and he preferred to leave it with her, in case of an emergency.

She felt Tye's forehead for what seemed like the hundredth time. Last time she'd checked, his temperature had been 100.1. He was rather prone to fevers; as long as it didn't go much higher or last too long, she didn't think there was much to worry about.

But still.

Joe should have called.

Her bladder twinged, reminding her that she'd been postponing a trip to their tiny bathroom for fear of disturbing Tye. She couldn't wait much longer. With a suppressed sigh, she gripped the windowsill and clung to the baby with her other arm as she got to her feet. He was finally putting on pounds now that he was eating table food. This last growth spurt alone seemed to have added five pounds. She doubted it was that much, but he did seem like a little brick these days. She would find out how much he weighed at his next wellness check.

Thank goodness their shoddy insurance at least paid for that. They didn't seem to cover much else.

When Tye didn't stir, she carefully laid him down in his crib. He immediately rolled onto his tummy with a noisy sigh. She eased a thin blanket over his rump, her fingers lingering against his back. She never realized how much someone could love a little person who couldn't say more than one or two words. *Dada* and *car* were the only things he said with enough consistency to count. She longed for the day when he said *Mommy* for the first time. It just didn't seem fair that she spent twenty-four hours a day with him, and he still didn't call for her by name.

She smoothed his dark hair away from his damp brow before turning to dart toward the bathroom while she had the opportunity. Just then, footsteps stamped outside the door. She paused as a key rattled the lock. A gust of cold air swept through the room as the door swung open and admitted a thin young man in a hoodie. Joe smiled at her as he closed the door and locked it behind him. He turned the deadbolt before sliding his hood back. Rain speckled his pale cheeks, dripping around the acne that plagued him, probably thanks to the grease and heat he endured at the restaurant. The smell of taco meat filled the room.

"You're late," Marian said, wrinkling her nose against the odor. She'd ask him to shower as soon as he finished his dinner, and she'd put his clothes in a plastic bag to mask the odor until she could get to the laundromat.

"Sorry." He slipped out of his nonslip-soled shoes and kicked them onto the mat beside the door. "Donny asked me to stop by on my way home."

At the mention of her cousin Donny Sheridan, Marian's mouth turned down, but when she replied, she spoke softly. "Couldn't he have waited until tomorrow? It's really late, Joe."

He glanced at her, brows pulling together as he lifted a black trash bag she only then noticed and dropped it loudly onto the floor. "Aliza gave us some more clothes for Tye." He sounded defensive, annoyed even, as he referenced Donny's older sister Aliza.

Marian's momentary annoyance gave way to guilt. Donny and Aliza were her cousins, and although she may not care for Donny, who happened to be Joe's best friend, she adored Aliza and appreciated her giving them her kids' hand-me-downs.

Still, Joe could have called. "Tye's had a temperature all night." She grabbed the bag and dragged it toward their tiny kitchen table so she could go through it.

Joe's mouth turned downward. "Again? Did you give him the baby Tylenol?"

Marian winced. "No. We're all out. I gave him a bath though, and that helped a little. He's sleeping now."

He nodded as he dropped carelessly onto one of the wooden chairs at their table. It groaned in protest but thankfully didn't dump across the floor in a pile of wood splinters. "I'm so hungry," he murmured as he leaned his head back, stretching it slowly from side to side as if to ease a hidden pain.

Was his stomach all he ever thought about? Already he seemed to have dismissed Tye's needs in place of his own. Marian knew she should be more sympathetic—he'd been on his feet for the past nine hours working in the steamy restaurant kitchen. He probably *was* exhausted. She knew that, but her annoyance didn't want to be appeased.

"There's a bowl of oatmeal in the fridge," she said. Her bladder reminded her that she still hadn't seen to her own needs. "I'm sorry, but I need to go to the bathroom."

His noisy sigh filled the apartment as she darted toward the toilet she so desperately needed. Well, what did he expect? A steak dinner? She couldn't remember the last time they'd had meat or fresh vegetables in the house. They hadn't been able to get groceries in nearly three weeks. There wasn't much left in the cupboards besides oatmeal, noodles, and rice.

He knew that as well as she did.

She exhaled in relief as she dropped onto the toilet seat to relieve herself. Her stomach cramped slightly, reminding her that girl time might be on its way. She'd been lucky so far. Since she was still breast feeding Tye, her periods hadn't really come back on a regular schedule yet. She'd only had two since Tye had been born, and they'd been very light and easy. Something she didn't mind one bit.

No periods meant she didn't have to worry about paying for birth control or marking dates on the calendar.

She checked the toilet paper, but there was no sign of an approaching period. Maybe she'd be lucky, and it would skip another month. She was nearly out of feminine products anyway. She couldn't afford to have a period until pay day. Maybe her body would behave itself and wait for a more convenient time.

One could always hope.

Saturday morning finally arrived, which meant Joe's paycheck was safely in their wallets. He trailed behind her with Tye in the cart as she led the way with the grocery list.

"What about yogurt?" Joe called. "We haven't had yogurt in a long time."

"It's not on the list." She mumbled the words as she perused the toilet paper on the opposite side of the aisle. Nothing was on sale, so she grabbed a 12-pack of the store brand. Hopefully it would be enough to last two weeks.

She turned to drop it into the cart in time to catch the look of severe disappointment on Joe's face as he stared gloomily at the dairy to their left. Guilt gnawed at her stomach, but what was she supposed to do? She could only make the budget stretch so far. Still, she walked around him to study the shelves of yogurt. The store brand was 25% off, so she grudgingly grabbed a tub of strawberry yogurt and set it into the shopping cart. She could do without creamer this week; the powdered milk in the back of the pantry would do for another month.

Joe beamed at her as if she'd just handed him a big bag of chocolates.

She couldn't help but feel a little happier. Sometimes she felt like she lived with *two* kids.

This wasn't what she had expected marriage to be like. They'd been married for about six months, and sometimes she still felt as if she were playacting in a high school drama. The plain gold band on her finger felt too loose even after Joe had it resized, like it didn't really belong to her. She used her thumb to spin the ring in circles, around and around as her thoughts swirled in similar patterns.

Parenthood. Marriage. Adulting.

It kind of stank.

She loved Joe and Tye, but this real-life stuff, with bills and fevers and crappy minimum wage jobs…they didn't put that kind of stuff in the marriage brochure. If it hadn't been for Tye, she often wondered if she and Joe would have gotten married. Sure, they'd been in love, but kids from her high school seemed to fall in and out of love like they were window shopping.

Their phone vibrated in her pocket. Still lost in her own thoughts, she tugged it from her jeans and glanced at the caller ID. She shot a panicky look at Joe.

"It's my folks," she muttered.

Joe's expression remained carefully neutral. "You can answer if you want."

Marian winced and glanced down at the vibrating flip phone. She loved her parents, but they'd made it clear in no uncertain terms that they did not approve of Joe as her choice of a life mate. Her dad especially had been unusually severe on the subject. He thought Marian could have done a lot better.

"I'll call them back later." She stuffed the phone into her back pocket and let the call go to voicemail.

Joe followed her silently down the aisle. When she stopped to grab a carton of eggs, he cleared his throat. "You know, maybe we should try a little harder with your folks. Invite them to come see us or something. They've only seen Tye maybe twice since he was born."

Marian's hands froze around the cardboard carton. There was no maybe about it. Her parents had only seen their first grandchild twice in his whole life. Sure, Dad's new job had taken him to Colorado shortly before Tye was born. They'd wanted Marian to move with them.

But she'd refused to leave Joe behind.

So they left without her, and she moved in with Joe and his buddy Frank, who'd since found a new roommate.

"They know where to find us," she finally said as she

chose her eggs and closed the door. Goosebumps trailed up and down her thin arms. She caught a glimpse of her own reflection in the glass: stringy pale hair, eyes hugged by dark circles, cheekbones too prominent as if she hadn't enough skin to cover them properly.

What was her dad thinking? She wasn't a prize catch herself.

"I know," Joe continued, oblivious to the turn of her thoughts. "I just don't want Tye growing up without knowing his grandparents, you know?"

Marian kept her eyes downcast as she turned and placed the eggs on top of the toilet paper, safely nestled against the side of the cart where they wouldn't get smashed. "At least he has Grandma and Papa Carpenter," she said, the words barely more than a murmur.

For a moment, she imagined she could see Joe's intense gaze studying her, but then she turned away, and he let the matter drop. She knew he wouldn't forget the conversation, though; once he got an idea into his head, he mulled it over again and again and wouldn't let it go.

They finished shopping and headed for the parking lot, toward their ancient car. Tye giggled and clapped his gloved hands as the automatic doors slid apart to release them to the dreary autumn day. A bitter wind slapped Marian in the face as she tugged her thin hood over her pale hair and stuck her hands in her pockets. An unpleasant mixture of rain and snow pelted the blacktop, so Joe steered the cart down the covered sidewalk in front of the strip mall. She plodded behind him, watching her battered tennis shoes as they slapped against the damp sidewalk.

Joe slowed down in front of her. She sidestepped and kept walking, lost in her own thoughts. It took a moment before she realized he was no longer moving forward. Turning to see around the edge of her hood, she saw him several yards behind her, staring intently at a storefront. Something about the way he seemed fixated made her a little uneasy. She followed the direction of his gaze to a simple array of glass windows, several functional signs covering the glass.

It seemed to be some kind of military recruitment office. She scrutinized the signs more intently. Army, by the looks of it.

Something unpleasant churned in her stomach.

"Joe?" When he didn't answer, she cleared her throat and called again, more urgently, a strange sort of panic stirring inside her. "Joe!"

His head snapped in her direction, his expression momentarily dazed, as if he couldn't remember where he was.

"Are you coming?"

Joe flashed her a slight smile, laughed, and spurred the cart forward. "Sorry, I'm coming." She waited as he crossed the sidewalk to catch up.

Although he said nothing about the store, she caught him glancing over his shoulder as they left the shelter of the awning and moved across the slushy parking lot. The sky glowered above them, and Marian couldn't help but feel as if eyes hungrily chased them toward their car.

Note from the Author

"For the LORD has called you like a wife
deserted and grieved in spirit,
like a wife of youth when she is cast off,
says your God.
For a brief moment I deserted you,
but with great compassion will I gather you."

Isaiah 54: 6-7

I have to thank AnnMarie Pavese for bringing this passage to my attention on the very day I sat down to write my Author's Note. I was honestly dreading the task, because to write this note requires a lot of introspection, a lot of digging deeper into a condition I wish didn't exist: Infertility. But more importantly, I have had to ask the question we all ask but fear to voice out loud: How can a loving God allow such painful things to happen?

When God first laid this story on my heart, I had no plans to actually sit down and write it. It was the second week of December. There was no possible way I could write, edit, and publish a story before Christmas in that amount of time.

Was there?

I fought His gentle urging for three days before I sat down to actually write *The Innkeeper's Wife*. I wrote all but the final scene in one day. I don't think I have ever been able to do that before IN MY LIFE. I sent the story out the next day to two of my beta readers. They both responded within 24 hours with raving reviews and great suggestions for improvement. Those of you in the writing world will know how incredible that is…most readers take much longer to work through a story, especially when they're preparing feedback. A day or two later I was able to make the necessary revisions, finish a cover, and get the story off to my editor.

For some reason, I feel like this story is meant to be out there. Someone, somewhere, needs to be reminded that they aren't alone.

Infertility is a subject that lays heavy on my heart. I have several family members and friends who cannot have children. To say I fully understand their pain is impossible, because…I just can't. God blessed me with my daughter two years ago, after struggling to become pregnant for several years. At the time, that felt like a long time. A long wait. We would love to have another child and have been trying for a year now. Another year that feels long to me but is nothing compared to the wait that others have gone through, that others are going through and will continue to go through. The disappointment that eats away at me each month can be so discouraging. This month, as I wrote this story, I tried to sit down and imagine how much heavier that pain must feel to someone who *doesn't* have a child already. To someone who doesn't have that comfort. Even if I can't ever have another child, I have my Evy. They don't have that.

I cried a lot writing this story. My own small, paltry emotions already feel so raw…but to add the pain of other women who don't even have what I have, all the Hannahs spread all over the world…this bit deep. This story was hard to write. It was hard to imagine such pain. It was hard to know that people I love live with this pain on a daily basis.

I'm so thankful that AnnMarie brought this passage to my attention. It captured the heart of the message I was hoping to convey in my little story. In AnnMarie's own words:

> "It's about God's promise to restore Israel,
> but it's told in the parallel of a woman
> who can't have children."

At first, I wondered how a promise could be compared to a woman unable to bare children. Where was the promise in that? Infertility is one of those "hopeless" things. It *feels* hopeless again and again and again, every month, like clockwork, a constant cycle of hope and disappointment that just repeats itself. It doesn't seem to end, and it certainly *feels* like it isn't going to end to the person trapped within the rotation. The person stuck watching the rest of the world move on, get pregnant, have children, while they remain fixed in a dark and lonely place.

So how is there a promise to the infertile woman in Isaiah 54? Verse one starts out by telling the poor woman to:

> "Sing, O barren one, who did not bear;
> break forth into singing and cry aloud,
> you who have not been in labor!"

My first reaction was: um…why? Why would she ever *want* to do that? In my humanity, in my weakness, I see no cause for rejoicing in being denied something that other woman are gifted so freely. I am so blessed to have my little girl, I cannot fathom life without her. I cannot fathom finding myself in a world without her, where I was told I couldn't have her, but that I still needed to rejoice and sing.

I think the promise comes in verse seven where God promises that, yes, he deserted her, but he only left her for a moment. For a season. Then, he draws her back in, gathers her back to himself with other promises—a nation of children that will endure. A nation of children that will see the Son of God walk on earth. A nation of children that will be blessed by *knowing* God intimately.

Are there not always two sides to every coin? For every shadow, there must also be a light source. For every valley, a mountain. For every tear, a shoulder to cry on. The hope lies in knowing you are not alone. You are not abandoned. You are not forgotten. That God has a great purpose for your life that will endure.

> "These I will bring to my holy mountain,
> and make them joyful in my
> house of prayer;
> their burnt offerings and their sacrifices
> will be accepted on my altar;
> for my house shall be called a hour of
> prayer for all people."

> Isaiah 56:7

The prayer of my heart goes out to all you women who struggle with infertility, to those I love, and to those I've never met. I cannot fathom your pain. But I hope you are reminded today that GOD CAN. He knows your pain. His altar is always open for you to bring your tears and pleas. Your voice will be heard. Your pain will be felt. Your sorrow will be shared. His door is always open, and in His time, He can and will bring you joy in the darkness.

> "For you shall go out in joy and be led
> forth in peace..."

> Isaiah 55:12

*All passages taken from the ESV translation.

Acknowledgments

Nicole, I want to thank you for taking the time to explain to me your perspective of infertility: from the ground floor, where it's really happening. This isn't something a lot of people talk about, but I'm so thankful you've opened up your heart and risked sharing what is inside.

I also want to give a huge shout out to my girls: Tammy, AnnMarie, and Sarah, who took time out of their busy schedules to help me polish up this story. I couldn't have done it without you sharing your personal stories, without your gentle guidance and enthusiastic fangirling.

Selina, thanks for squeezing in a last-minute proofreading job, and for going above and beyond to point out some other things as well that helped to make this little story shine.

Lastly, I'd like to say thank you to the women who inspired this book—the girls with empty arms and big dreams. Hang in there and don't give up hope. This story is for you.

Thanks

If you enjoyed this story and want to make every day Christmas for the author, please don't forget to leave a review on Amazon and Goodreads as a small thank you.

Also Available by Savannah Jezowski

The Neverway Chronicles
"Wither" in *Five Enchanted Roses*
After
Specter

When Ravens Fall Series
When Ravens Fall
Well of Fate

Timeless Nativity Series
The Innkeeper's Wife
The Carpenter's Wife

The Whitby Tales
Curse and Consequence
Magic and Mischief (Coming 2020)

The Witching Hour Series
The Witching Hour
Hound of Darkness

Short Stories
"Well of Fate" in *Mythical Doorways*
"Tears of the Sea" in *Tales of Ever After*
"The Witching Hour" in *Paws, Claws, and Magic Tales*

Non-Fiction

On My Own: How to Format Your Ebook and Print Layout in Microsoft Word

Poetry

"Various poems" in *For the Love of a Word*
"Out of the Sea" in *A Kind of Death*

About the Author

Savannah Jezowski lives in southern Michigan with her Knight in Shining Armor and two wee warrior princesses. She studied Commercial Writing/English in college and eventually founded Dragonpen Press, a small publishing house that offers author services such as cover design, developmental edits, and interior formatting. Savannah specializes in fantasy and Christian fiction with colorful and dimensional characters and likes to deal with emotional themes. She is also featured in six different anthologies such as *Five Enchanted Roses* and *A Kind of Death*. When she isn't writing, Savannah likes to read books, watch BBC miniseries, and play with cover designs. She also enjoys having tea with her imaginary friends.

Want to know about sales and new releases? Sign up for Savannah's newsletter at www.dragonpenpress.com.